Lion's Lunch

Written by Hiawyn Oram

Illustrated by Woody

Lion and Tiger were in their cave.

"I want my lunch," said Lion.
"Then go out and get it,"
said Tiger.

"It's too hot to go out," said Lion.
"Well then," said Tiger, "I will get
your lunch for you."

Tiger went outside.

Soon he saw Hare coming along.

"Hello, Hare. Have you heard? Lion is sick."

"Oh dear, can I help?" said Hare.

"Why not go to see him?"
said Tiger.
"OK," said Hare, and he went
into the cave.

Then Deer came along.

"Hello, Deer. Have you heard? Lion is sick," said Tiger.

"Oh dear, can I help?" said Deer.

"Why not go to see him?"
said Tiger.
"OK," said Deer, and she went
into the cave.

Then Fox came along.

"Hello, Fox. Have you heard?
Lion is sick," said Tiger.
"Oh dear, can I do anything?"
asked Fox.

"Why not go to see him?"
said Tiger.
"Yes, why not?" said Fox,
and he went up to the cave.
But then he stopped.

"Hang on," said Fox. "Look at these footprints going into the cave. There are none coming out!"

"So?" said Tiger.

14

"I'm not going!" said Fox.
"If I went into that cave
I'd soon be..."